Zahra's Blessing
A RAMADAN STORY

WRITTEN BY **Shirin Shamsi**

ILLUSTRATED BY **Manal Mirza**

Barefoot Books
step inside a story

The silver moon hung like a sideways smile.

"It's the Ramadan moon, Teddy," Zahra whispered. "Mama says blessings are all around us during this month. Maybe Ramadan will bring a sister for me. And we'll make crescent cookies together."

A prayer rose from Zahra's heart like a sigh and floated up into the starry sky.

"Can I help?" Zahra asked.

"Sure," Mama said. "I'm collecting clothes to donate."

"But you love that jacket," Zahra said. "And my hat from Auntie."

"You outgrew that hat two years ago," Mama said. "And there are people who need the jacket more than I do."

"Baba says we get more blessings when we give," Zahra remembered.

Mama smiled. "Baba is very wise, but we should give without expecting anything in return."

"Maybe my Ramadan blessing will be a sister!"

"Insha'Allah," Mama said. "We must wait and be patient."

"Mama, Baba, have you seen Teddy?" Zahra asked.

Her parents shook their heads.

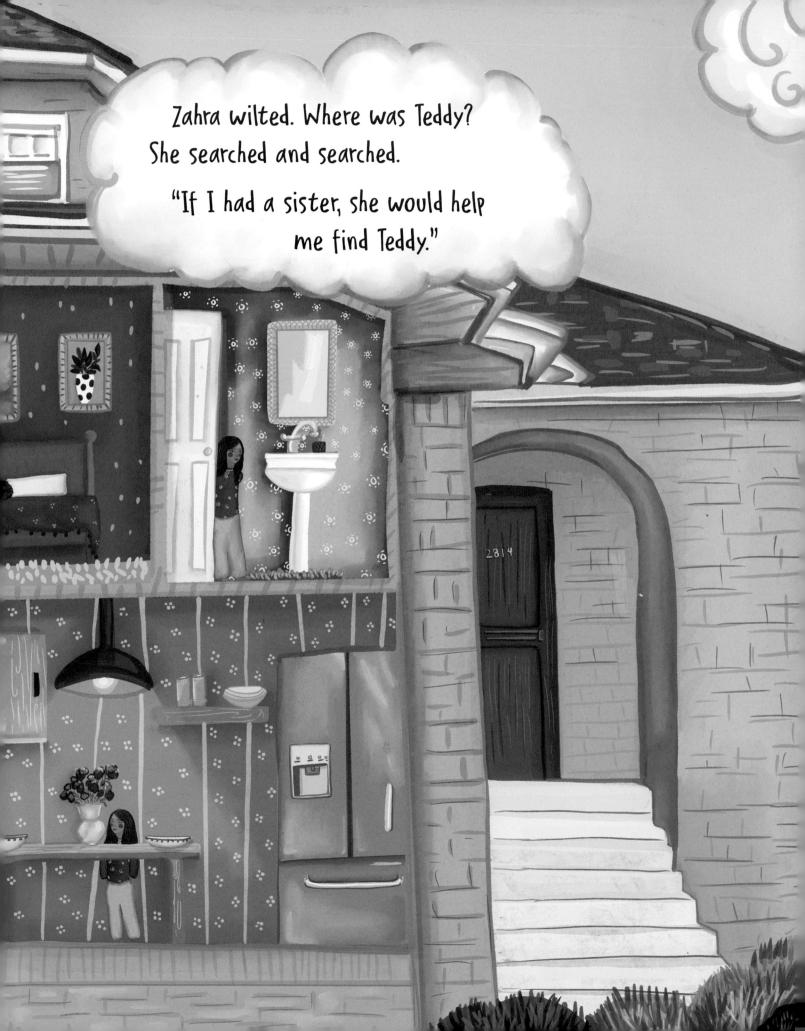

Zahra wilted. Where was Teddy?
She searched and searched.

"If I had a sister, she would help
me find Teddy."

Night fell and iftar came.

Mama prepared all the foods Zahra loved best for breaking the fast.

Scrumptious samosas, delicious dates and refreshing rooh-afzah!

"I pray I find Teddy," Zahra whispered. "And a sister." Her heart fluttered between sadness and hope.

The following day Mama took Zahra
with her to volunteer at the shelter.

"The people here come from other countries,
where they lost their homes," Mama explained.
"They are living here for now, until the shelter
can help them find places to stay."

"Is that why we gave them our boxes
of clothes?" Zahra asked. Mama nodded.

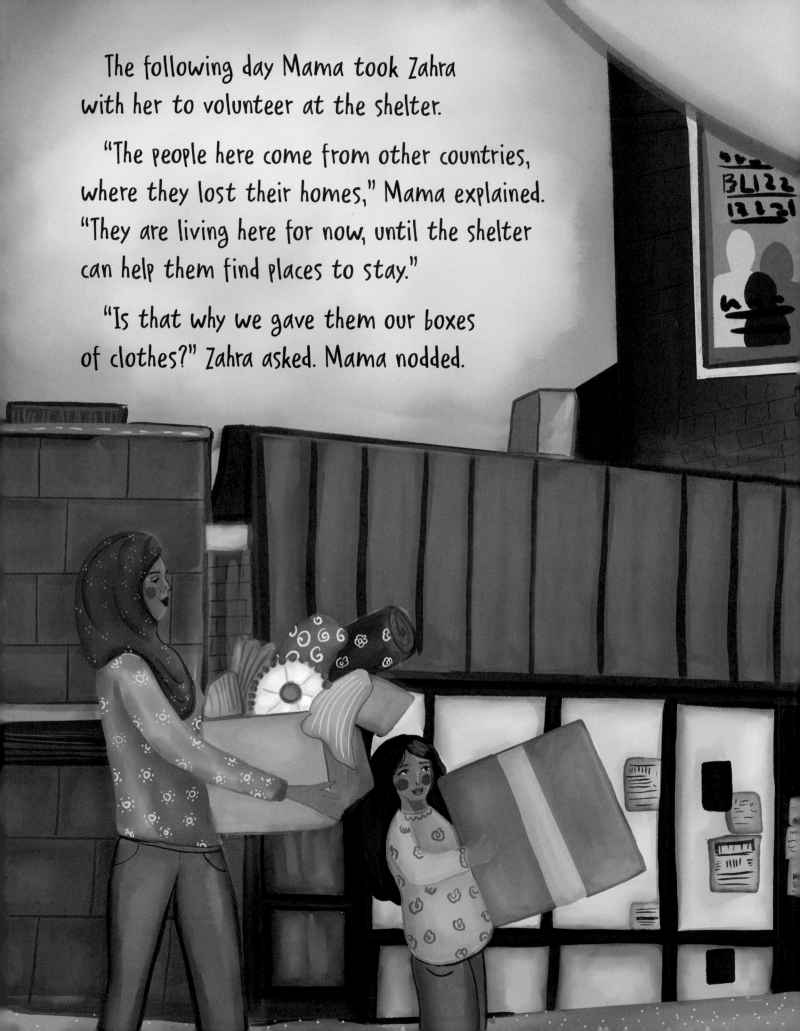

Zahra's heart hurt from losing Teddy.

But the people here had lost everything.

Their hearts must be hurting too, Zahra thought.

Mama said, "Zahra, while I help prepare iftar, I'd like you to meet someone special. This is Haleema."

"Your picture is beautiful," Zahra said shyly.

"My baba was an artist," Haleema said. "Do you want to paint with me?"

Zahra sat down and Haleema showed her how to paint tall mountains with sunlight dancing over them. "Like where we used to live," Haleema said.

After they painted, Haleema asked Zahra to read to her.

"I love stories about wizards and dragons," Haleema said.

"So do I!" said Zahra.

They read and talked until iftar time. Then they ate together and shared desserts.

At last, Mama said, "It's time to go home."

Haleema's eyes held a sadness that was deeper than an ocean.

More than ever, Zahra wished that she had Teddy back ... so she could give him to Haleema.

Some days of Ramadan crawled like a snail, while others skipped like a squirrel.

There was fasting by day and praying by night.

Zahra visited Haleema at the shelter. They built big, busy block cities.

"My mama was an architect!" Haleema said. "Someday I want to build skyscrapers like she did."

At night, Zahra still missed Teddy. But now she thought about her new friend too.

Finally, it was the night before Eid.

That night, Baba and Mama wrapped Zahra into their arms.

"We have something special to tell you," Baba said.

Zahra loved being in the middle of a Mama and
Baba sandwich ... but not as much as she loved
the news Baba whispered in her ear.

Eid Day dawned dazzling bright.

Zahra's dress glimmered and glowed bright as her smile, for she carried a special secret in her heart.

Crowds of brightly dressed people gathered in the mosque for Eid prayers and greeted friends. "Eid Mubarak!"

Back at home, Zahra organized and decorated. She took out all her best blocks and dragon books.

Will she like it? Zahra wondered.

The doorbell rang.

Zahra ran to answer it.

When Haleema unpacked her belongings, Zahra gasped.

"What?" Haleema asked.

Zahra's heart felt full, as she looked from Haleema to Teddy. He must have fallen into the clothes donation box all those weeks ago!

Zahra smiled. "It's just that I've been praying for this for so long."

"Really?" Haleema hugged her new sister. "Me too!"

They did not need to search for blessings,
for blessings came from all around.

And the silver sliver of moon winked down at them.

RAMADAN

Zahra and Haleema celebrate Ramadan, a special time of year for Muslims. It is the ninth month of the Islamic Lunar Calendar, which is based on the cycles of the moon. Ramadan is considered the month of the Quran *(kur-AHN)*, the holy book of Islam. During this holy month, people focus on God, patience, gratitude, self-control and giving to others.

EID AL-FITR

Eid al-Fitr *(EED al-FIT-ur)* is the holiday at the end of the month of Ramadan. Believers hope that their practices during the month of fasting have strengthened their relationship with God, improved their willpower and softened their hearts.

On Eid al-Fitr, the community gathers together for the Eid prayer in the mosque or in a large open space. Families and friends share meals, parties and gifts, and often eat lots of sweets.

FASTING

During the days of Ramadan, from dawn until sunset, those who are physically able will fast. Fasting means to not eat or drink, but it also includes avoiding hurtful words or actions. People spend time doing good deeds and studying the Quran.

Every day at sunset, people gather for iftar, to break (end) the day's fast together with food. At night, people gather in the mosque or in their homes and spend time in prayer. At the end of the month, families give charity, called zakat al-fitr *(za-KAT al-FIT-ur)*, to complete their offering to God before celebrating Eid.

DISPLACEMENT

People become displaced if they have to leave their homes to find safety. This can happen anywhere in the world. It could be because of a natural disaster, like a flood or a fire, or lack of food or jobs. Or it could be due to violence, like war, or when a minority group is being harmed. Sometimes people have to leave their homes and go to other places in their own country. Other times, people leave their country to seek asylum or refuge (protection) in a different country where they will be safer. These people are called asylees or refugees. Of the world's displaced people, 40% are children.

SHELTERS

A shelter helps displaced people adjust to life in a new country. They may need help with understanding the language, finding a place to live and completing government paperwork. Displaced people are often forced to leave most of their belongings behind when they leave their homes, so shelters may also provide food, clothing, toys and household items that people need to start rebuilding their lives. Lawyers, interpreters, caseworkers and social workers all help do these jobs.

FOSTER CARE

Community members and volunteers — like Zahra and her family! — can play an important role in welcoming asylum seekers and refugees to their new homes, jobs and schools. If a child is not with family members when they are displaced, they may need a foster family to care for them. Long-term foster care placement is a slow and careful process. Zahra's parents would have applied to become a foster family for a child like Haleema well before the beginning of this story.

For Talha, my greatest blessing! – S.S.

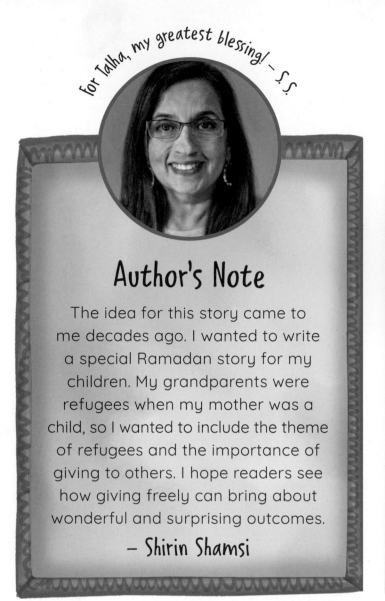

For all my nephews and nieces, who inspire me daily – M. M.

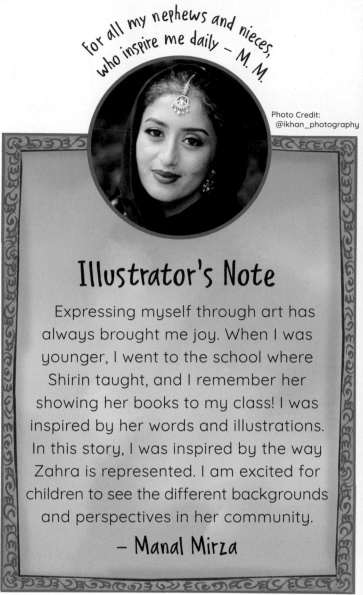

Photo Credit: @ikhan_photography

Author's Note

The idea for this story came to me decades ago. I wanted to write a special Ramadan story for my children. My grandparents were refugees when my mother was a child, so I wanted to include the theme of refugees and the importance of giving to others. I hope readers see how giving freely can bring about wonderful and surprising outcomes.

– Shirin Shamsi

Illustrator's Note

Expressing myself through art has always brought me joy. When I was younger, I went to the school where Shirin taught, and I remember her showing her books to my class! I was inspired by her words and illustrations. In this story, I was inspired by the way Zahra is represented. I am excited for children to see the different backgrounds and perspectives in her community.

– Manal Mirza

Special thanks to the following people who helped bring this book to life:

Autumn Allen, EdM, MA, MFA | Kaitlin Roberson, EdM, Immigrant and Refugee Advocate

Mallika Iyer, Asia Programs Coordinator and Humanitarian Action Specialist, Global Network of Women Peacebuilders

Barefoot Books
23 Bradford Street, 2nd Floor
Concord, MA 01742

Barefoot Books
29/30 Fitzroy Square
London, W1T 6LQ

This book was typeset in Delivery Note and Quicksand
The illustrations were painted digitally

Hardback ISBN 978-1-64686-493-5
Paperback ISBN 978-1-64686-494-2
Spanish paperback ISBN 978-1-64686-518-5
E-book ISBN 978-1-64686-567-3
Spanish e-book ISBN 978-1-64686-568-0

First published in the United States of America by Barefoot Books, Inc
and in Great Britain by Barefoot Books, Ltd in 2022

Graphic design by Sarah Soldano, Barefoot Books
Edited and art directed by Lisa Rosinsky, Barefoot Books
Reproduction by Bright Arts, Hong Kong
Printed in Malaysia

British Cataloguing-in-Publication Data: a catalogue record for
this book is available from the British Library

Library of Congress Cataloging-in-Publication Data
is available under LCCN 2021043352

1 3 5 7 9 8 6 4 2